Galactic Holiday: The North Pole Awakens

Gabriel Snowboy

Gabriel Snowboy

Copyright © 2025

All Rights Reserved

Dedication

For my late son Colin.

This book is, and always will be, for you. It is a story that would never have existed without your spark. Your incredible imagination was the seed from which these words grew, and your memory was the quiet encouragement that pushed me to the final page.

Your spirit is woven into the very fabric of this story, living on in its characters and its heart. It is my deepest hope that every reader will find a piece of themselves reflected in these chapters.

This book is also dedicated to all those who, like him, see the world differently. It is for the dreamers and visionaries who bravely share their vision, helping the rest of us reimagine the world and make it a more interesting and compassionate place.

My son was one of those rare people. He shared an imaginative vision that inspired our small community to strive for improvement. He taught us to face the trials of life head-on, to understand the consequences of inaction, and above all, to be true to who we are.

May we all learn to enjoy this life as he did and have the courage to reimagine the world for the good of all.

Acknowledgment

I am deeply grateful to everyone who helped bring this story to life.

My deepest gratitude to the entire team at Author's Eden for their professionalism and passion.

To my wife, Anita, my love and inspiration. I cherish your patience, belief, and the love you poured into our family during the long hours of writing. This journey would not have been possible without you. My heart is yours, always.

I must also thank my amazing parents. Thank you for your lifelong love and support.

And to my beautiful kids, you are my greatest inspiration. Thank you for the joy and laughter you bring into my life every day; your understanding and support gave me the extra push I always needed.

Finally, to you, the reader. Thank you for picking up this book and spending your time with these characters and this world. I hope you enjoyed the journey.

Table of Contents

About the Author

Gabriel Snowboy is a member of the Cree Nation of Chisasibi, a community located in the vast territory of Eeyou Istchee at the end of the road in northern Quebec. His commitment to his people has defined his career, first as a carpenter who helped build homes for the community and later as a public servant.

A dedicated family man, he works hard to support his wife, Anita, and their six children. This dedication to family and community inspired him to become a key figure in the self-sustaining northern agriculture movement, helping to inspire a new way of life for the Cree Nation. Today, Gabriel Snowboy continues his service by working for the Cree Nation Government.

This book is an extension of his commitment to his community. He hopes his journey will inspire others to build, nourish, and serve their communities for generations to come.

Chapter 1

The Dream

Far from the known world, beyond mountains and seas, lay a hidden village steeped in joy. Lanterns glowed in frosted windows, laughter echoed between cottages, and magic hummed faintly in the air. This was the North Pole, where elves worked tirelessly, snow never ceased to fall, and the Christmas spirit lived in every heart.

Yet beneath the snowdrifts and merriment, the North Pole carried a secret. One so heavy it threatened to shatter the world should it ever surface.

At the village's center stood the largest house of all, its roof crowned with icicles like fangs. Before it rose a towering Christmas tree, adorned with thousands of lights. Inside, warmth pulsed from a blazing hearth.

Santa Claus lowered himself into his massive chair at the head of the table, the wood creaking beneath the weight of centuries. Though his beard was long and white as snow, his frame carried the strength of a man who had weathered countless winters. His crimson coat was not merely festive; it was stitched with ancient patterns of gold thread, runes, and swirls that whispered of a power older than memory —a mantle handed down through generations of Santas. His eyes, though softened with warmth, held a depth that suggested he had seen both wonder and sorrow alike.

Across from him, Mrs. Claus set down steaming plates with practiced grace. Her gown carried the same woven symbols, though hers gleamed with softer colors: emerald and silver, patterns that spoke of hearth and home rather than command. Her face was round and kind, her smile carrying a comfort that could melt the harshest winter storm. If Santa was the mountain, firm and immovable, Mrs. Claus was the hearth-fire, steady and welcoming. Together, they filled the great house with both majesty and warmth.

"This looks delicious, Mrs. Claus," he said, eyes twinkling.

"Thank you, Santa." She smiled, though her gaze flicked toward the stairs. "But where is Duke? Supper grows cold."

"He's outside, playing with his friends. Some game they've invented." Santa chuckled.

Mrs. Claus frowned. "That boy had better come inside soon."

Outside, the games raged on. Snowballs flew in every direction, children laughing and shrieking as they ducked behind icy barricades. Duke crouched beside the last of his teammates, his cheeks flushed from the cold, his small frame half-buried in the snowbank. He was the youngest in the group. Smaller, quicker, not yet as strong as the older children. Yet his eyes burned with a focus none of them carried.

While the others had fallen one by one, Duke refused to yield. His heart pounded, not with fear, but with a fire that drove him to rise where others faltered. Even in play, courage carried him forward, as though something deep inside him whispered he was meant for more than games.

"It's just us now," the older boy said. "I'll distract them. You flank them."

Duke nodded. He crawled along the snowbank, shaping four quick snowballs with numb fingers. Then, springing from cover, he struck one, two, three hits. The enemy team toppled in defeat.

"We won!" Duke shouted, triumph ringing in his voice.

But his celebration ended as Mrs. Claus's voice cut through the night.

"Duke! Supper's ready!"

He winced. "Oh no…" He turned to his friends. "Sorry, I've got to go."

Moments later, Duke burst through the door. "I'm sorry, Mom! I forgot about supper."

"And you'll forget it entirely if you don't sit and eat," Mrs. Claus interrupted, placing a warm plate before him.

Santa winked. "Even milk and cookies are a feast when she makes them."

Later, in his room of toys and unopened presents, Duke changed into his pajamas. Just as he climbed into bed, a knock came. Santa entered, sitting on the edge of the mattress.

"Did you have fun today?"

Duke smiled. "Yeah. It was amazing."

"Good," Santa said softly. "Because one day, Duke, you'll take my place. Being Santa is more than giving gifts. It is a burden—and a gift greater than any other."

Duke blinked. "Me? But you're already the best Santa."

Santa chuckled, though sorrow shadowed his eyes. "There are things I wish I could have changed."

"Like what?"

"Tomorrow," Santa said. "I'll tell you tomorrow."

As the door closed, Duke whispered to himself, "How could I ever be Santa?" His eyes drifted shut.

Sleep swallowed him.

Duke dreamed.

The world around him twisted into fire and ruin. Flames devoured the village, their glow bleeding into the endless black sky. Smoke clawed upward in choking spirals, blotting out the stars. The houses, once filled with laughter, buckled and collapsed, their roofs crackling as if screaming in agony. Toys lay shattered in the snow, melting into ash as the fire swallowed them whole.

At the center of it all lay Nicholas, still and lifeless, his red coat torn and burned. Beside him, Mrs. Claus clung to his body, her sobs carrying through the roar of the inferno.

Duke stood frozen, his chest tight, his throat raw. Sadness struck first, sharp and hollow, pulling tears to his eyes. But beneath it, something hotter swelled anger, fierce and uncontrollable. His fists clenched as if he could tear the fire itself apart, as if he could strike down whatever force had brought this ruin. Yet no matter how hard he tried to move, he remained rooted, powerless, forced to watch as everything he loved turned to ash.

A voice echoed in the darkness: Well done.

Duke stumbled into a mirror. His reflection was no longer a child, but an older man cloaked in shadows, eyes glinting coldly. Behind him loomed a blurred figure.

My son…

The glass shattered.

Duke jolted awake, lungs burning as if he'd carried the smoke back with him. His nightclothes clung damp against his skin, slick with sweat. For a moment, he lay still, heart hammering in his ears, until a flicker at the window caught his eye. He turned, seeking the calm of the snowy night beyond… and froze. Outside, in the drifting snow, a toy soldier sprinted away from the factory. Another toy chased after it, panic in its tiny face.

Chapter 2

The Stranger in the Storm

Duke pulled on his coat and slipped outside. The cold bit instantly, sharp against his cheeks, the wind driving flakes into his eyes. Ahead, the two small figures darted through the snow, their shadows stretching long across the drifts. Teeth clenched, Duke lowered his head against the storm and followed them up the hill, each step heavier than the last.

"Stop!" he called. "What's happening?"

The toy soldier whirled, voice high and breathless. "Strange folk hooded ones. They stormed the factory. Broke everything."

Duke's blood ran cold. "What?"

He sprinted back toward the village. But the air reeked of smoke, and orange flames licked at the horizon. Houses burned. Entire families had vanished. Yet Santa's house stood untouched, looming in eerie silence.

"Santa!" Duke shouted, rushing inside. The rooms were empty. Mrs. Claus was gone. Santa was gone.

He stumbled back into the snow, voice breaking. "Anyone? Please!"

Silence answered.

He collapsed to his knees, tears stinging his eyes. "They're gone…"

Duke crested the hill, breath ragged in the cold. The little figures had stopped, their tiny forms trembling in the snow. Most of them broke away, scurrying toward the shadows of nearby cottages in search of shelter. But one stayed behind.

It was an action figure, no taller than Duke's hand, its painted armor dulled by frost. Slowly, it stepped forward through the snow, cautious but determined, until it stood before him. Its head tilted back to meet his gaze, eyes glinting faintly in the moonlight.

"Forgive me… but I was told to find you, to take you somewhere safe. You are Master Skyrider."

Duke looked up, stunned. "Skyrider? No, I'm Duke."

The toy's gaze held steady. "You are Duke Skyrider. The one we were made to protect."

Duke's heart pounded. The name struck him harder than the cold. Skyrider. He had always believed he was Santa Claus's boy, raised beneath the weight of that name. But now the word echoed in him, heavy and unfamiliar, as if a door had been opened, he never knew existed.

"Skyrider…" he whispered, the sound strange on his tongue. For the first time, he realized he might not be who he thought he was.

The village smoldered behind him. With nothing left, Duke followed his strange companions into the storm.

Snow blinded his path, the wind shrieking in his ears.

"Straight ahead!" the toy shouted above the gale.

At last, the storm broke, revealing a cavern of glittering ice. Stalactites hung like frozen spears. The walls gleamed with a faint, unnatural glow.

Duke stepped inside, shivering. "There's nothing here."

A low rumble stirred the cave. Snow shifted, piling, rising.

A voice whispered: "Wrong."

Before Duke's eyes, the drifting snow began to gather, swirling into a shape that rose taller and taller. Ice cracked and groaned as it fused, the form hardening into the body of a snowman. But this was no child's creation. His body was built of ancient ice, edges jagged and weathered by storms long past. His surface glistened like glass in some places, rough and scarred in others, as though time itself had carved him. Within his sockets burned a faint blue light, steady and watchful, like embers trapped in frost.

The snowman's mouth curved into a weary smile. His voice rumbled, deep and resonant, carrying the weight of centuries.

"Call me Frosty."

Duke's breath caught. His fists unclenched as the name hit him.

"Frosty… Santa spoke of you. He said you were the one who showed him how to use Christmas magic… that you made him the Santa he is today."

Frosty's gaze lingered on him, the glow of his eyes flickering like candlelight in the wind. For a moment, he looked haunted, as if the memory carried both pride and pain.

"Long ago," Frosty said slowly, "before the dark days. I taught Nicholas what he needed to become who he was meant to be. And now…" He leaned closer, frost shedding from his frame in brittle shards. "Now, boy, I will teach you."

Duke swallowed hard, heart racing. "If this is the only way to save him… then teach me."

Frosty tilted his head, studying him. "Curious… your training begins just as his did."

"His?" Duke asked.

Frosty's gaze lingered on Duke, the ancient blue glow in his eyes flickering. His voice dropped, heavy as stone cracking under ice.

"They began here… their training. Nicholas… and his brother."

The cave seemed to grow colder at the words, the frost around them groaning as if it remembered. Duke stiffened, his breath catching in his throat. Santa has a brother?

Frosty's eyes dimmed, and for a moment, he looked as though he wished he could take the words back.

Chapter 3

Frost and Fire

The cave seemed to exhale a cold so sharp it bit through Duke's coat. Frosty loomed above him, crystalline arms glittering in the dim light, his voice like the grinding of ice.

"Santa had a brother once," Frosty said, his eyes narrowing. "Few remember him. Fewer still speak his name."

Duke's breath clouded in the frigid air. "Why not?"

"Because the spirit of giving did not bind his heart, but by envy. Where Santa was chosen to bear the gift of Christmas Magic, his brother coveted it. He sought to twist it, to wield it for power."

The boy swallowed, his chest tightening. "What happened to him?"

Frosty's gaze darkened. "He was banished. Or so we thought."

A silence fell, broken only by the faint drip of melting icicles. Duke's fingers trembled, not from the cold this time, but from the weight of what he had heard.

The action figure at his side piped up, almost cheerfully. "And now, Master Skyrider, Frosty will train you. You must learn the magic before the brother returns."

"Train me?" Duke blinked. "I don't even know where to begin."

Frosty's great head tilted. "You will. Magic is not found in spells or charms. It is born from within, from the will of the heart. But first, you must learn discipline."

He lifted one massive hand. A swirl of snow lifted from the cave floor and hardened into three spheres of ice. They spun in the air between them.

"Catch them before they fall," Frosty commanded.

The spheres dropped at once. Duke lunged, fumbling, and two slipped through his hands, crashing to the ground in splinters—the third he caught, barely.

Frosty's eyes gleamed. "Not hopeless."

Duke scowled. "That wasn't fair."

"Nothing is fair," Frosty rumbled. "The enemy will not play games with you."

The toy soldier leaned on Duke's boot, looking up. "Best do as he says, Master. He's been here since the first snowfall."

Frosty's ancient frame creaked as he turned deeper into the cave. "If you would learn, you must endure. And if you endure, perhaps then… perhaps you may even find your parents. They may yet live."

The words struck like a hammer. Duke's heart lurched into his throat. His parents are alive? He didn't wait for another breath, another word. His legs moved before thought, pounding through the snow toward the village.

"Duke, wait!" the toy soldier shouted, scrambling after him, his tiny feet slipping in the drifts. Frosty groaned, shards of ice breaking from his body as he gave chase, his booming voice rolling after the boy.

But Duke didn't stop. He couldn't. If there was even a chance…

Chapter 4

The Burning Village

Hours slipped away in the storm. Duke ran until his lungs burned, the snow blinding his eyes, but still he pushed on. Behind him, the heavy crunch of Frosty's steps and the frantic patter of the toy soldier's boots never stopped, always chasing, constantly calling his name.

When at last the boy crested the final ridge, his legs buckled beneath him. The storm had thinned, the air eerily still, but the sky ahead glowed a sickly red.

The village was still burning. Flames licked through broken rooftops, sparks clawing into the night. Ash drifted like black snow, coating the once-bright streets in a blanket of ruin. Even after hours, the fire had not died.

Frosty caught up, his ancient frame shuddering, shards of ice cracking loose from his shoulders. The toy soldier stumbled to Duke's side, voice small and strained.

"It… it shouldn't still be burning."

Duke's chest tightened until he could barely breathe. The place he had known, its warmth, its music, its glow, was nothing but ruin.

He stumbled a step forward, shaking off Frosty's heavy, icy hand. The snow hissed under his boots, blackened by ash. Homes sagged in charred heaps, their beams still smoldering. Where the grand Christmas tree had once towered in the heart of the square, only a blackened trunk jutted from the snow, its strings of lights melted into silence.

And then he saw it.

Santa's chair was dragged into the square, overturned, and blackened by fire.

"Santa!" Duke cried, his voice raw. "Mom!"

No answer. Only the wind.

Frosty's voice came like thunder. "Do not linger here. The enemy may still be close."

Duke spun on him, tears blazing in his eyes. "I can't just leave them! They're my parents!"

The snowman's gaze softened, though his jagged mouth never moved. "You are not strong enough yet. If they live, they are taken. If they are taken, there is still hope. But only if you endure."

Duke's fists balled at his sides. The soldier toy tugged gently at his sleeve. "Listen to him, Master. Please."

Through the smoke, Duke thought he saw movement, a hooded figure slipping into the shadows of a ruined house. He froze. The air seemed to thicken, a presence pressing against his chest.

And then it came, a sound low and hollow, curling through the air like smoke. It wasn't speech, not fully, but it pressed against his mind, heavy and cold, as if the night itself were whispering. The same echo from his dreams. The same chill that sank beneath his skin and would not let go.

He turned to Frosty, his voice breaking. "Did you hear that?"

But Frosty was staring into the dark, his eyes like frozen fire. "He is closer than I feared."

The snowman bent low, his vast hand lowering toward Duke. "Climb on. There is no time left. If you remain, you will be found."

Duke hesitated only a moment before scrambling onto Frosty's shoulder. As the snowman rose to his full towering height, the ruined village shrank beneath them. The fire crackled, the smoke carried, and somewhere in the shadows, unseen eyes followed.

Chapter 5

Ashes of Joy

The snow crunched beneath Duke's boots as he slid down from Frosty's shoulder. Smoke still rose from the ruins, curling through the night like black fingers. The village that once sparkled with laughter and lantern light now lay in silence, broken and charred.

He stepped forward slowly, as though walking through a dream. The wooden stalls where elves had once sold toys were now nothing but smoldering skeletons. The bakery, where sweet smells had once drifted out each morning, had collapsed into ash. The air reeked of smoke and something fouler, something that didn't belong to fire or wood.

Duke's breath trembled. "Why would anyone… do this?"

Neither Frosty nor the toys answered.

He reached the town square. The Christmas tree that had towered over the celebrations was blackened and fallen, its ornaments shattered across the snow like bloodied jewels. Santa's great chair lay on its side, half-burned, as though dragged there for some cruel purpose.

Duke fell to his knees. "They're gone. Everyone's gone."

Frosty loomed behind him, silent. His shadow stretched over the boy like a great, jagged wing.

Then Duke heard it again.

Well done…

The voice slithered into his ears, deep and smooth, echoing from no single direction but from everywhere at once. The air grew heavier, colder, though the fires still burned.

Duke's heart raced. "Who's there?"

A figure moved in the smoke. Cloaked in black, its hood drawn low, it stepped with calm precision into the square. Others appeared behind it, small shapes, twisted like elves but wrong. Their faces were hidden, their hands clutching jagged shards of wood and metal.

The first figure raised its head slightly. Beneath the hood, Duke glimpsed only the faintest gleam of pale skin and eyes like frozen coals.

"Ah…" The voice purred, the same one from his dream. "The boy."

Duke staggered back, his throat dry. "What do you want?"

The hooded one tilted its head. "What was promised. What must be claimed."

The twisted elves behind it hissed softly, their movements jerky, unnatural, as though strings pulled them.

Frosty stepped forward, ice cracking beneath his bulk. His voice rumbled with ancient fury. "Back. You have no place here."

The hooded figure laughed, low and steady. "Still guarding secrets, old snow? You cannot shield him forever."

Duke looked up at Frosty, panic flooding him. "Who is he?"

Frosty did not answer.

The figure took another step, the firelight flickering across his cloak. "The boy will come to me. It is already written."

The toys clung to Duke's coat. The action figure whispered fiercely, "Master, we must go!"

The figure extended a pale hand from his cloak. The fires surged higher, twisting into shapes, faces screaming in the flames, eyes wide with torment. The broken ornaments on the ground glowed like embers, pulsing with unnatural light.

Duke's chest tightened until he could hardly breathe.

Frosty bent swiftly, scooping the boy into his icy palm. "Enough." His voice thundered through the square. "You will not take him tonight."

The figure's eyes glowed brighter under the hood. "Then tomorrow."

The fire roared, and when Duke blinked, the figure was gone. Only the ruined square remained, ash drifting like falling snow.

Frosty turned, his voice low. "We must leave, Duke. Now."

The boy could not speak. He only clung tighter as the snowman carried him away, the burning village shrinking behind them.

Yet in his heart, Duke knew: the voice would follow.

It already lived inside his dreams.

Chapter 6

The First Lesson

The snowstorm swallowed the burning village until it was nothing but a faint glow on the horizon. Duke buried his face in Frosty's icy palm, refusing to look back. The fire's light still danced in his mind, the hooded figure's words echoing in his ears: The boy will come to me.

They walked until the night stretched into pale dawn. At last, Frosty stopped at the edge of a frozen plain, where jagged peaks rose like teeth around a hollow.

"This will do," the snowman rumbled. He set Duke down gently on the snow. "You will begin here."

Duke shivered. His breath smoked in the air. "Begin what?"

"Your training," Frosty said. "If you would survive what hunts you, you must learn the magic that has guarded this land since the first winter."

The boy frowned. "But I don't have any magic."

"Wrong." Frosty's eyes gleamed like twin shards of ice. "Magic is in you. It is in all Santas-to-be. But to awaken it, you must control your fear. If fear rules you, then he will claim you."

The words chilled Duke more than the wind.

The toy soldier tugged on Duke's sleeve. "You can do it, Master. We'll help."

Duke looked down at him, really seeing him for the first time, the scuffed paint, the dent in his helmet, the fierce determination in his tiny face.

"What's your name?" Duke asked.

The toy stiffened. "Name?"

"Yes." Duke managed a small smile. "You've been helping me since this started. You can't just be 'toy soldier.'"

The toy hesitated, then straightened proudly. "I am Nico, sir. Built to protect, sworn to follow. But tonight, I choose to stand with you."

Duke felt warmth stir in his chest, faint but steady. "Thank you, Nico."

Frosty's voice thundered. "Good. Trust in your companions. But now you must learn to harness the light."

He raised one great hand. From the snow, an icy pillar rose, smooth as glass. Its surface shimmered faintly with an inner glow.

"This," Frosty said, "is a focus crystal. It will draw out what lies within you. Place your hands upon it."

Duke stepped forward, heart hammering. The pillar's cold seared his palms. At first, nothing happened. Then, slowly, a warmth stirred deep in his chest, pushing against the cold.

The crystal pulsed faintly.

Nico gasped. "It's working!"

But suddenly, the warmth twisted. The voice returned, curling in Duke's mind: Well done…

The crystal's glow darkened, shadows writhing inside it. Duke staggered back, clutching his head. "No! Stop!"

Frosty's arm slammed down between him and the pillar. Ice cracked like thunder. "Focus! The darkness feeds on your fear. Control it—or be consumed."

Duke fell to his knees, gasping. His hands shook uncontrollably.

Nico scrambled up onto his shoulder, gripping his collar. His tiny voice rang clear, sharp against the suffocating dark.

"Master, hear me. That voice isn't yours. It wants to unmake you, twist you into something you're not. But I've seen who you are. The one who saves, even when destroying, would be easier. The one who carries light when everything else falls into shadow. That's you. Don't let it take that away."

Duke's eyes locked on the tiny figure. Nico's voice cut through the storm in his head. He clenched his fists, pushing back the whispers. The glow inside the crystal shifted again—darkness cracking, light bursting free.

For a heartbeat, the pillar blazed with pure radiance. Snow around them glittered like diamonds.

Then it dimmed, and Duke collapsed, panting.

Frosty loomed over him, studying with unreadable eyes. "Not hopeless. But you are unready."

Duke wiped his brow, breath still ragged. "I… I saw him again. The man in the cloak."

Frosty's mouth curved downward, jagged teeth catching the light. "You will see him more. He will press against your mind, your dreams, your fears. That is his power."

"Who is he?" Duke whispered.

Frosty's silence stretched, heavy as stone. At last, he said: "The one Santa never wished you to know."

Duke looked down at Nico, who still clung to his collar. For the first time, he didn't feel entirely alone.

Chapter 7

The Brother's Name

The frozen plain stretched silent around them, wind whispering like voices of the dead. Frosty loomed, his gaze heavy on Duke, as if weighing whether to speak the truth.

At last, the snowman's chest heaved with a sound like cracking glaciers.

"You have asked who he is. Then hear it and know the danger you face."

Duke steadied his breath, Nico's tiny hand still clutching his collar for courage.

"Santa," Frosty said, "was not always called Santa. He was born Nicholas, a boy like any other but blessed by the ancient spirit of Christmas. From him flowed the magic that gives joy, that bends time and space to deliver wonder to every soul."

Frosty's jagged mouth curved downward, sorrow glinting in his icy eyes.

"But Nicholas was not alone. He had a brother, older by only a winter. His name was Gabriel."

The name struck Duke like a blow. He had expected something monstrous, but not this. Gabriel, so human, so ordinary.

"Gabriel desired the same gift that Nicholas was given. When the spirit chose Nicholas, Gabriel's heart turned black with envy. He swore that if he could not bear the magic of Christmas, then no one would. He would see the joy his brother brought twisted into despair."

Frosty's voice deepened, carrying the weight of centuries.

"Their battle raged across these snows long ago. Nicholas triumphed, but he could not bring himself to destroy his brother. Instead, he cast Gabriel into exile, binding him beneath the endless storm. We thought him gone forever."

Duke's breath fogged before him. "But he's back."

"Yes," Frosty said. "The storm that breaks across these lands is his prison cracking open. He seeks you now, Duke."

"Me?" The boy's voice cracked. "Why me? I'm not even ready to be Santa!"

"You are Nicholas's heir," Frosty said simply. "The spirit chose him, and it has chosen you. That is why Gabriel whispers in your dreams. He seeks to turn you before you understand your strength. If you fall, the North Pole falls with you."

The weight of the words pressed on Duke's chest like stone. He looked down at Nico, his voice small.

"What if I fail?"

The toy soldier stood tall upon his shoulder, saluting despite the tremble in his painted hand.

"Then you get back up, Master. Because failure is not defeat until you give up. Nicholas never gave up, and neither will you."

Frosty bent lower, his icy breath swirling around them.

"The first lesson was control. The second will be endurance. You must hold your light against the storm. Gabriel will not wait. He will come for you soon."

Duke clenched his fists, heart pounding. Nicholas, his father, had carried this burden. Now it was his.

"Then teach me," Duke said. His voice trembled, but it did not break. "Teach me everything."

Frosty's jagged smile gleamed.

"So be it."

Chapter 8

The Gift of Fire and Light

The cavern grew darker as the storm outside howled, its fury pressing against the icy walls. Frosty's crystalline body shimmered faintly, his jagged arms folded as he towered over Duke.

"The storm is not wind alone," Frosty said. "It is Gabriel's hate. It seeps into your bones, weakens your will. To fight him, you must carry your own fire and never let it die."

Duke stood trembling, his breath harsh in the frozen air. Snow clung to his hair, his gloves soaked through. His legs shook from hours of drills running in circles, forcing his body to push against walls of ice and lift heavy blocks until his arms burned.

"I can't..." he gasped, sinking to his knees. "I can't do this anymore."

"You can," Frosty's voice thundered like cracking glaciers. "The question is not can you, but will you."

Nico clambered down from Duke's shoulder, standing in the snow like a tiny soldier on the battlefield. His painted face was calm but firm.

"Master, Nicholas trained harder than this once. Frosty nearly broke him, too. But he endured. Because he knew what waited if he failed."

Duke clenched his jaw. The dream clung to him like ash, flames, ruin, emptiness. A shiver crawled down his spine.

From somewhere deep within, a voice coiled through him, cold as ice.

Well done…

His breath caught, hollowed out as if the night itself had stolen it.

He forced himself to rise, arms trembling. "I'll keep going."

Frosty nodded once, the snowstorm inside the cave swirling tighter. "Then we move to the final trial."

The snowman raised his arms, summoning a cyclone of frost and ice. The cavern floor cracked, lines of frozen energy racing outward like veins of lightning. The air burned with cold.

"You must shape the magic within you," Frosty said. "The spirit lives in your blood. Call it forth. Make it obey."

Duke shut his eyes, his heart hammering. He stretched out his hands, but nothing happened. His palms were numb, useless.

"Feel it," Frosty urged. "It is not in your muscles. It is not in your breath. It is in your heart, Duke. The fire of Christmas. The joy that gives, not takes. Focus!"

The boy strained, teeth gritted. His breath came ragged, his chest tight with frustration.

"I don't feel anything!"

"You do," Nico shouted, voice high but fierce. "Think of the village. Think of Nicholas. Think of what you're fighting for!"

And then, a spark.

Duke's right palm flickered with a faint glow, as if a star had been caught in his skin. His eyes snapped open. The glow swelled, brightening, stretching, burning into a white-gold blaze.

With a cry, Duke thrust his arm forward. From his palm erupted a blade of radiant light, pure energy, humming with power—the cavern walls lit like fire, shadows fleeing from the brilliance.

The weapon burned in his grasp, extending outward like a sword made of molten frost and golden flame. His hand did not blister, did not freeze. It felt… right.

Nico staggered back, eyes wide.

"By the bells of Christmas… he's wielding the Light of Nicholas."

Frosty's jagged grin spread wide, awe rumbling in his voice.

"Yes. The spirit has chosen. The boy has forged the Blade of Joy."

Duke stared at the glowing weapon in his hand, his chest heaving. The hum of the light pulsed in time with his heartbeat. He raised it higher, the glow casting him not as a child, but as something greater.

"Gabriel will come for me," Duke said, his voice steady now. "And I'll be ready."

The blade flared brighter, as if it agreed.

Chapter 9

The Speed of Santa

The cavern had become Duke's world. Days blurred together, endless echoes of his blade humming, Frosty's commands booming like thunder, Nico's sharp voice pushing him forward.

The weapon of light answered his will now. He could summon it with a thought, its golden blade snapping alive in his palm, heat and frost swirling together. Frosty tested him relentlessly: forcing him to strike moving targets of ice, to cut boulders as they tumbled toward him, to block shards of frozen spears hurled from the snowman's jagged arms.

Frosty's voice dropped lower, heavy as falling snow.

"Long ago, when the brothers trained, Nicholas mastered it in only days. He moved with joy, laughter carrying him faster than the wind itself. He could outrun the night itself, racing ahead of the darkness so dawn would always follow in his wake. His gift was born of wonder, of selflessness."

Frosty's tone hardened.

"But Gabriel… Gabriel could not surrender to joy. His heart was heavy with envy, and every attempt left him slower, weaker. It took him months to grasp it, and even then, it was fueled by anger, not wonder. His power was heavy, desperate, and nothing like Nicholas' light."

Duke swallowed hard, the image of two brothers—one outrunning night, the other chained to shadow, burning in his mind.

Frosty's eyes glowed like shards of ancient blue ice.

"The Speed of Santa."

Nico stepped forward, nodding solemnly. "The magic that let Nicholas cross the entire world in a single night. Faster than storms, faster than fire, faster than fear itself."

Duke's heart pounded. He thought of his dream, of the burning houses, of Gabriel's whisper. If he had that speed, maybe he could stop it.

"How… how do I use it?"

Frosty's ancient form loomed in the cold cavern, the cracks in his icy frame glowing faintly with frost-blue light. His voice rumbled like shifting glaciers.

"Your gift is not just in your hands, Duke. You must let it flow through your whole body. Every breath, every muscle, every step. Pour the magic into yourself and run."

Duke clenched his fists, sweat already stinging his brow despite the freezing air. He nodded, planted his feet, and bolted into the tunnel. At first, it was nothing more than his boots pounding against ice, his lungs burning with each gulp of air. The tunnel's shadows stretched endlessly, mocking his effort.

"More!" Frosty commanded, his voice echoing down the cavern. "You're holding back. Release it!"

Duke focused, trying to push the strange warmth in his chest outward, down his arms, into his legs. For a moment, he felt lighter, faster, but then the power sputtered out. He stumbled, slammed to the ground, and gasped for breath.

He dragged himself back up, refusing to quit. Again, he ran. Again, he fell. Hours passed, his body aching, his chest tight, his throat raw from icy air. Time blurred; the cavern floor was littered with the marks of his endless sprints.

Still, Frosty pressed him.

"Again, Duke! Until the magic obeys you—not the other way around."

Nico's small voice cut in, strained with worry. "You can do this! Don't stop now!"

Duke staggered, then forced himself forward, tears freezing at the corners of his eyes. Each stride, he willed the magic to move, to spread through him. His heart thundered, his body screamed, yet some hidden spark deep inside refused to give way.

He ran. And ran. And ran.

"Faster, Duke!" Nico shouted from behind. "Faster!"

The walls around him blurred. The sound of his boots began to echo not as steps, but as a constant rushing roar. The tunnel stretched and twisted, yet he flew through it, faster than his own eyes could follow.

And then, the world snapped.

Light bent around him, streaks of silver and gold flashing across the ice. He no longer felt the ground beneath his feet, only the rush of wind tearing past, his heart beating with impossible rhythm. He was moving so fast, the air cracked like thunder in his wake.

"Ha!" Duke shouted, exhilaration flooding his chest. "I'm doing it!"

He burst from one end of the cavern and reappeared at the other in less than a heartbeat. Again. Again. A blur of red and white streaks through the cave. The sound of bells seemed to ring faintly with every step, as though the world itself was singing with his speed.

Frosty's jagged mouth curled into something like a smile. "Yes… he has it."

Duke skidded to a halt before them, chest heaving, steam rolling from his lips. His entire body glowed faintly now, traces of golden energy flickering along his arms and legs.

Nico gazed up at him in awe. "The Blade of Joy in your hand… and the Speed of Santa in your blood. Gabriel doesn't stand a chance."

Duke looked down at his trembling hands, then clenched them into fists. His fear was still there, but something more substantial now pulsed beneath it. Resolve.

"Then let him come," Duke said, voice steady. "This time, I'll be ready."

The cavern fell silent, save for the whisper of the storm outside as though even the blizzard was holding its breath.

Chapter 10

Shadows in the Snow

The cavern had grown quiet again, save for the soft hiss of Duke's breath. His body still hummed with energy, golden sparks crawling over his arms as though lightning slept beneath his skin.

He could feel it now, this new power, the blade at his command, the speed of Santa pulsing in his veins. When he closed his eyes, he imagined the world before him: fires to quench, enemies to crush, even Gabriel himself falling before his hand.

"I could end this," Duke whispered. "I could stop Gabriel before he takes another step. Before he even knows I'm there."

His words echoed through the cave.

Nico's small plastic hands tightened around the hilt of his toy sword. He looked uneasy. "Careful, master. That's the same way Gabriel once spoke."

Duke's eyes flickered to him. "What do you mean?"

The action figure's voice grew heavy, though it was still small. "Gabriel was once like you, chosen, gifted. He, too, learned the blade of light. He, too, ran at the speed of Santa. But he looked at his power and thought, 'I am unstoppable. I am greater than Nicholas.'"

Frosty's massive body shifted, ice cracking beneath his weight. His voice rolled low, like thunder in a storm.

"Gabriel forgot what the gift was for. He believed the power belonged to him, not to the world. And that belief twisted him. The faster he ran, the deeper he fell into the shadows."

Duke clenched his fists. "I'm not Gabriel. I'm not going to fall."

The snowman's glowing eyes bore into him.

"Everyone who falls says the same, boy. It is not hatred that tempts you. It is certain. The moment you believe you cannot fail… is the moment the shadows find you."

Duke turned away, breathing hard. But the words crawled inside him.

Because part of him, the stronger, bolder part, whispered back: Maybe Frosty's wrong. Maybe Gabriel just wasn't strong enough. But I am.

The cavern seemed colder then.

Nico stepped closer, his plastic face solemn. "Master… power without restraint is a fire in a blizzard. It does not warm, it only consumes. You must listen."

Duke tightened his jaw. "I'll listen. But when Gabriel comes… I won't hold back."

Frosty's jagged mouth curved into something between a frown and a warning grimace.

"You must learn, Duke. The true strength of Santa is not speed. Nor blade. It is the joy he carries, even when the night is darkest. Lose that… and you are already Gabriel."

Silence fell. The cave pulsed with a low wind, whispering like a thousand voices in the snow.

Duke lowered his head, though his fists still burned with golden light. He wasn't sure if he was agreeing with Frosty… or silently arguing with him.

Chapter 11

The Storm Breaks

The storm that had trapped them inside the cavern for days finally began to subside. What once howled like wolves against the ice faded to whispers, and pale sunlight broke through a ceiling of gray clouds.

Duke stepped out first, his breath forming a plume in the cold morning air. The snow stretched for miles, broken only by the trail of smoldering ruins to the north, towards the village. His village.

Nico hopped down into the snow beside him, landing with a slight crunch. "The path is open. We should move quickly. If Gabriel's followers struck, they may have left a trace."

Frosty loomed behind them, his shoulders glistening with frost. "Aye. But remember, boy," he said, his cold gaze fixed on Duke. "This is not a hunt for vengeance. You are searching for Nicholas. To find him, you must walk with joy in your step, not wrath."

Duke nodded, though inside his chest a storm still raged. The visions of fire, the memory of his dream, the blade that hummed in his hand, they pushed him toward anger. But he recalled Frosty's warning, and Mrs. Claus's smile at the supper table. *Joy,* he told himself. *I have to bring happiness. Even here.*

The village was not as he left it.

Wisps of smoke curled from collapsed roofs. Icicles hung like teeth from half-burnt doorframes. Toys lay broken in the snow, their bright colors dimmed beneath ash. And yet, among the ruin, Duke's speed allowed him to move carefully, quickly, lifting beams as he searched for survivors and pulled out what unbroken toys he could salvage.

A group of cracked and scorched wooden soldiers fluttered their painted eyes open as Duke set them upright. "Go on," Duke whispered to them, forcing a small smile. "Stand tall again."

They straightened, their wooden feet clacking on the cobblestones, saluting him faintly. For the first time, Duke felt the weight in his chest ease. His power hadn't been destroyed. It had been restored.

Frosty watched from the edge of the square. "Better," the snowman rumbled. "You are learning. To wield the gift is not to dominate, but to lift."

Nico scampered toward a darkened doorway, pointing. "Here! I've found something!"

They followed him into what had been the toy workshop. The air smelled of charred pine. On the floor, seared into the wood, was a symbol: a spiral of thorns curling into a crown.

Frosty froze. His voice dropped low, as if speaking to himself. "Gabriel's mark."

Duke crouched, staring at it. His hand trembled, sparks threatening to ignite from his fingertips. He clenched his fist tightly. *Restraint. Joy. Don't give him what he wants.*

"They took Santa this way," Nico said, his feeble voice tense with fear. "They left their sign so that we'd know. So that you'd follow."

Duke stood, the blade of light humming faintly at his side, though he hadn't summoned it. He could feel the trail ahead, like a cord pulling him into darkness.

"Then I'll follow," he said quietly. "But not with hate. With hope. We'll bring him back."

His words lingered in the smoke-filled air, fragile yet luminous, like a candle burning against the endless dark.

Chapter 12

The Beast of the North

The trail carved by Gabriel's followers led beyond the burnt village and into the white wilderness. The snow stretched uninterrupted, and the silence was broken only by the crunch of Duke's boots and Nico's hurried little steps.

"Stay sharp," Frosty warned. "Gabriel does not leave marks for you to follow without traps."

They pressed on, the cold intensifying around them until the air itself felt heavy, pressing against their lungs. And then, the silence cracked.

A deep rumble shook the snow beneath their feet.

From the edge of a frozen ravine rose a shape taller than houses, its fur white as the storm and eyes glowing like frozen lanterns. Massive claws dug into the ice as it pulled itself free, its roar rolling across the empty tundra.

"The Frostbeast," Frosty muttered grimly. "Born of the North Pole itself. A guardian spirit twisted by Gabriel's corruption."

Duke's blade of light sparked to life in his hand, humming with energy. The Frostbeast lunged, snow bursting apart as its paw crashed down where he had stood a heartbeat earlier. Duke's speed carried him clear, the world slowing around him as he darted across the beast's flank. He slashed upward, carving a searing arc across its arm. But instead of blood, shards of ice sprayed into the air.

The beast bellowed, out of pain and fury. Its eyes glowed brighter, blue fire spreading through the cracks in its body.

"Duke!" Frosty's voice cut through the chaos. "Do not kill it!"

Duke froze mid-strike, blade raised. "What? It's trying to tear us apart!"

"Because it suffers," Frosty replied, standing firm as the monster roared again. "Santa would never destroy one of his own guardians. He would heal it. Save it."

Duke's chest heaved. The urge to finish the fight surged through him, the power humming at his fingertips begging for release. But Frosty's words ran deep. Santa would save.

The beast lunged again. This time, Duke didn't swing his blade. He dropped it, letting the light fade, and raised both hands instead.

He thought of the children's laughter in the village. He remembered Mrs. Claus's gentle smile, Santa's warm chuckle, and joy itself, pure and bright. He let it spill out.

Light burst from his palms, not sharp like a weapon but warm and radiant. It encased the Frostbeast in a golden shroud. The cracks in its icy body began to seal as the fire in its eyes dimmed, leaving only a pale blue glow.

The beast collapsed into the snow, breathing heavily, then raised its massive head toward Duke. For a moment, boy and creature shared a silent gaze, not of enemies, but of kin. Then it let out a low rumble, bowed its head, and slowly trudged back into the white wilderness.

Duke fell on his knees, panting, the snow steaming around his hands. "I… I almost killed it."

Frosty knelt beside him, his icy hand heavy on the boy's shoulder. "And in choosing not to, you proved yourself closer to Nicholas than to Gabriel."

Nico stepped forward, eyes wide with awe. "Master… you saved it."

Duke looked at his hands, still softly glowing with golden sparks. "Saved it…" he repeated, half in wonder, half in fear.

Because the power had felt even stronger when he held back.

Chapter 13

Trials of Restraint

The Frostbeast's shadow still haunted Duke's mind as they pressed deeper into the frozen expanse. The snow fell more softly now, no storm to obscure their sight, but the silence felt heavier than ever, as if the land itself was holding its breath, waiting.

Nico trudged at Duke's side, small legs working furiously to keep pace. "Master, the way you calmed the beast… it was unlike anything I've seen." His voice carried both awe and unease.

Frosty moved forward, his icy form crunching through the snow. "Remember, boy. Power can kill, but restraint saves. Nicholas learned this lesson too late. Gabriel never did."

Duke nodded, though his hands still trembled from the memory of holding back. *If I had struck… Nico could've been safe faster. One swing. One strike. Done.*

That thought poisoned his chest. But he shoved it away.

The trail wound through jagged spires of ice, tall as towers. Their sharp edges caught the moonlight, glowing pale blue. It was here that the subsequent trial struck.

The air shimmered, and from the spires emerged twisted shapes. Shadow-elves, cloaked in tattered garments, their eyes glowing red. Illusions, yet solid enough to kill. They swarmed suddenly without warning.

"Stay behind me!" Duke shouted, his blade sparking to life. He moved with Santa's speed, weaving between them in blurs of light. His strikes didn't kill, not this time, but shattered their forms into drifting shards of shadow.

One by one, they vanished.

Then a scream.

"Nico!"

The boy turned too late. One shadow-elf had slipped past him, driving its jagged blade straight for the toy soldier.

Duke's world froze.

He *could* end it with a strike. He felt the power surge within him like fire, desperate for release. But if he let it go unchecked, if he unleashed the full force, he might not just destroy the elf. He might destroy everything within reach.

"Duke!" Frosty's voice cracked the air like thunder. "Restraint!"

The decision tore through him. Rage urged him to end it. Fear begged him to save Nico at any price. But Santa's words echoed in his mind: Bring joy, not ruin.

Duke let the fire flickered. He reached out not with the blade, but with the light within him. His speed surged, carrying him faster than thought. He was there in an instant, his hand between Nico and the shadow. Golden sparks burst, not to destroy, but to push the elf back. It shattered, dissolving into the cold night.

Nico tumbled into the snow, gasping. His painted chest bore a crack, but he lived.

Duke dropped beside him, his heart pounding. "I almost—" His throat tightened. "I almost lost you."

Nico coughed, and then managed a shaky grin. "But you didn't. You saved me without... without giving in."

Frosty loomed over them, eyes stern, but proud. "This is the path Nicholas walked when he was tested. The temptation to strike harder, faster, and crueler always lingers. Gabriel chose it. And it consumed him."

Duke looked down at his hands, still tingling with light. For the first time, he understood that restraint wasn't weakness. It was harder than any strike. Harder than giving in.

And it was the only thing preventing him from Gabriel's fate.

Chapter 14

The Trap of Shadows

The trail narrowed into a canyon of black ice. Frost clung to the jagged walls, and the silence grew unbearable. Duke's every step echoed like a drumbeat in a tomb.

Frosty's voice was quiet and cautious. "This place… I do not like it. Gabriel has walked here before."

Nico clutched his toy sword tighter, his crack from the last battle glinting faintly in the moonlight. "Master Duke, something's wrong. I can feel it."

And then the world shifted.

The canyon walls bent, melted, and before Duke stretched not ice but fire. Homes were burning. The North Pole village was engulfed in flames. Screams echoed through the air, and the stench of smoke choked his lungs.

"Mother!"

He saw her. Mrs. Claus lay in the snow, her red dress torn and her glasses cracked. Beside her, Nicholas himself, Santa, was pinned under the shattered Christmas tree, his chest still.

"Father! No!" Duke's blade sparked to life, wild with panic.

Frosty stepped into Duke's path, his massive hand pressing against the boy's chest. "This is not real. Do not give it power."

But the screams were too real. Nico's small hand tugged nervously at his sleeve, trembling. "Master, listen to him! It's a trap!"

And then came the voice. Smooth, cold, echoing through the fire.

"Why fight it, little Duke?"

From the smoke stepped a tall figure cloaked in shadows, eyes glowing faint crimson. His face bore echoes of Nicholas, but sharper and crueler, with mockery twisted into every smile.

Gabriel.

"You feel it, don't you? The weakness of restraint. They die while you hold back. They burn while you hesitate." He pointed towards Santa's broken body. "You could save them, if you only let go."

The fire roared higher. Mrs. Claus reached for him, coughing blood. "Duke… help us…"

Duke's blade hummed fiercely, his hand trembling. He could end it. End Gabriel, end the flames, end the torment. All it would take was one strike, one surrender to the raw fury in his veins.

"Do it," Gabriel whispered. "Unleash yourself. Be the Santa the world truly needs. Not weak. Not shackled by joy. A god of winter and death."

"NO!" Frosty thundered, ice cracking beneath them. "It is an illusion! If you attack with hate, you will give him your soul!"

Duke's vision blurred with tears. He could hear his parents' screams. He could *feel* their hands reaching for him.

He dropped to his knees, pressing his palms over his ears, struggling with the heaviness of it. "They're real... they have to be..."

Nico climbed onto his shoulder, gripping his collar with both tiny hands. His painted eyes burned with desperate faith. "Master Duke, remember what Santa said! *Bring joy, not ruin!* If you give in, Gabriel wins. And the real Nicholas is lost forever!"

Duke's breath shook. He raised his blade high. Gabriel's eyes gleamed with triumph.

Then, Duke let the blade vanish.

He pressed his hands together, whispering through his tears. "You're not real. You can't be. And I won't destroy myself trying to save shadows."

The fire wavered. Mrs. Claus's cry grew hollow. Santa's broken body turned to ash. Gabriel snarled, his form flickering.

"Foolish boy. Every restraint pushes you closer to failure. When the moment arrives, you will beg for my power."

And then he was gone. The canyon returned, silent and cold.

Duke sank into the snow, drained, his chest heaving. Frosty knelt beside him, voice gentler now. "That… was your hardest trial yet. Gabriel's whispers are poison. He knows where you are weakest."

Nico hugged Duke's neck, voice trembling. "But you resisted. You chose not to kill. Even when it hurt most."

Duke closed his eyes, a single tear freezing against his cheek. "If this is what it takes to walk Father's path… then I'll keep choosing restraint. No matter how much it breaks me."

Chapter 15

The Hall of Echoes

The canyon opened into a cavern. Its ceiling stretched high above, with crystalline ice glittering like a cathedral of glass. The silence inside felt heavy, broken only by the drip of melting frost.

Duke moved cautiously, his boots crunching against the frost-covered stone. His chest still ached from the illusion of the village burning, with the cries of Nicholas and Mrs. Claus haunting him like ghosts.

"Be cautious," Frosty murmured, his snowy bulk squeezing through the entrance. "This place… I have not seen it in centuries. It reeks of him."

Nico tugged Duke's sleeve nervously. "Master Duke, maybe we shouldn't—"

The cavern shuddered.

From every wall, voices spilled forth. Not Gabriel's voice this time. No, they were *familiar*.

"Duke…"

"You're too weak."

"You'll never be Santa."

"You'll fail just as Gabriel said you would."

The echoes emanated from the ice, each carrying the voices of people he knew —friends, elves, and even Mrs. Claus herself.

Duke's fists tightened. "No. They're lies."

But the cavern mocked him, shifting. The crystalline walls rippled like water, and suddenly, images appeared.

On the left: Duke, older, dressed in Santa's red robes. He stood proudly, but the children he delivered to turned away from him, frightened of his blade, his speed, his power. Their gifts lay shattered at their feet.

On the right: Nicholas himself, radiant and beloved, carrying a sack bursting with joy. The crowd cheered his name.

The voices grew louder, pounding against Duke's skull.

"He was the true Santa."

"You are nothing but his shadow."

"Gabriel is right. You will destroy more than you save."

Duke dropped to his knees, clutching his head. The ice mirrored his trembling face from a thousand angles.

"I'm not... I'm not a shadow..." he whispered, though even to his own ears, it sounded hollow.

Nico lunged in front of him, toy blade drawn, voice fierce despite his small size. "Master Duke, listen to me! These aren't truths. They're chains Gabriel forged for you. If you believe them, you'll forge the last link yourself!"

But Frosty's voice was grave. "And yet... illusions cut deeper than blades. Gabriel's trials are not to break his body but his spirit. If he falls here, all will be lost."

The cavern trembled again. From the shadows, Gabriel's form appeared, taller than before, his cloak of darkness rippling like smoke.

"You feel it, don't you?" His crimson eyes locked on Duke. "The weight of a crown is too heavy for a child. Nicholas gave you nothing but hope that will *crush you*. I offer release. Walk away from his path, and you'll never suffer again."

Duke forced himself up, legs shaking. His blade sparked weakly to life in his palm, though it wavered like a dying ember.

"You're wrong..." His voice cracked, but he stood firm. "Nicholas believed in me. Mrs. Claus believes in me. Frosty, Nico... they're still here. And that's enough to keep going."

Gabriel's smile curled cruelly. "Bravery in words, weakness in soul. Each step you take toward me, boy, I will strip away another piece of you. And when you are hollow, when there is nothing left but doubt, you will call me *father*."

The shadows surged, slamming into the walls, and in an instant, Gabriel disappeared.

The cavern grew silent. The voices faded away. The illusions dissolved back into raw, jagged ice.

Duke collapsed to the floor, drenched in sweat, his blade extinguished. His breaths were ragged, and his chest felt heavy.

Frosty bent low, placing a heavy snow-hand on his shoulder. "You resisted again, but each time it grows harder. He is not testing your strength, Duke. He is wearing it down."

Nico climbed onto Duke's knee, looking up at him with painted eyes that somehow shone with courage. "Don't let him in, Master. He wants to turn you into another Gabriel. But you're not him. You never will be."

Duke lifted his head, eyes wet with tears, but his jaw set with steel. "If Gabriel thinks he can break me with shadows, then he's forgotten one thing…"

He clenched his fist, his voice low and trembling but still defiant.

"Even in the dark, Santa brings the light."

Chapter 16

The Sundering Path

The cavern narrowed, funneling into a jagged tunnel of ice. Frosty's footsteps echoed like boulders rolling, while Nico's tiny feet softly tapped against Duke's shoulder. The boy's hands trembled as he held a faint glow from his blade, its light flickering on the frozen walls.

"Not much farther," Frosty rumbled. "The air tastes different here. I can feel the remnants of Nicholas's magic, but tainted."

Nico straightened up. "That means Gabriel must have come through this way!"

But the deeper they went, the thicker the shadows grew. Not just the absence of light, but *living darkness*, coiling across the walls like veins.

Duke swallowed hard. "Stay close. Something's wrong."

They turned a corner, and the path split.

Two tunnels yawned before them, mirror images, each pulsing faintly with a sickly red glow.

Frosty's coal eyes narrowed. "This is no natural formation. It's a rift. A trap."

The ground trembled. The glow intensified. Before Duke could react, the ice between the tunnels shot upward, forming a wall of blackened frost, slicing him away from Frosty and Nico.

"DUKE!" Nico screamed, pounding his tiny fists on the wall.

"I'm here!" Duke shouted, slamming his blade against it. Sparks flew, but the wall swallowed the light, absorbing the strike like it was nothing.

Frosty's voice boomed. "Hold strong, boy! Do not give him an opening!"

But then silence.

The voices were gone. Frosty's heavy footsteps faded. Nico's shouts muffled until they vanished.

Duke stood alone, his blade dim in the suffocating dark.

And then, Gabriel's voice slithered through the air.

"Alone at last."

The tunnel stretched before Duke, endless. The walls rippled like liquid, and from them stepped figures.

Mrs. Claus, weeping. Frosty, shattered into pieces. Nico, limp and broken.

Duke stumbled back, shaking his head. "No! No, you're not real."

Gabriel's voice coiled around him, heavy and personal. "Are you so sure? You've already seen them burn once, boy. How many times must you watch before you break?"

The illusions staggered toward him, whispering.

"You weren't fast enough!"

"You weren't strong enough!"

"You'll never save him!"

Duke clenched his fists, his blade flickering to life in a burst of raw fury. He slashed at the shadows, each swing cutting them down, but for every one that fell, two more rose, choking the tunnel with their accusing faces.

He screamed, swinging wildly, until the blade sputtered out. His chest heaved. His knees buckled.

Then came silence.

And out of the stillness, Gabriel himself stepped forth. Cloaked in shadow, eyes burning like coals in the dark. His voice was soft, almost gentle.

"This is what Santa never told you, Duke. Power doesn't save. Speed doesn't protect. Love doesn't endure. In the end, *everyone is taken from you.* Nicholas will die, as all things do. And when he does, you will stand where I stand now. Alone."

Duke's shoulders shook, and tears welled in his eyes.

But somewhere beneath the heavy weight of Gabriel's words, he heard something faint. Not Frosty's voice. Not Nico's.

His own.

Nicholas's promise whispered back to him, a memory. *'Being Santa is a gift greater than any other. You'll follow in my steps, and be greater than I could ever be.'*

Duke's tears dried as his breath steadied. He stood, raising his trembling hand.

The blade reformed. Not in fury this time, but in calm light, humming steady, warm.

"You're wrong," Duke whispered, his voice steadying. "I'm not alone. I carry them with me even if you try to tear them away."

The shadows recoiled. Gabriel's smile flickered, just for a second.

Duke stepped forward, blade blazing bright against the dark. Each step pushed the illusions back until the tunnel itself began to quake, shattering under the force of the light.

The wall behind him collapsed. Frosty and Nico hurried through, their voices piercing the silence like sunlight breaking through a storm.

"DUKE!"

He turned, breath ragged but eyes blazing. "I'm here."

The illusions were gone. The tunnels merged into one.

And beneath the rubble of the false path, something glimmered. A piece of crimson cloth, frayed but unmistakable. Nicholas's robe.

Duke knelt, lifting it in his hands reverently. His jaw clenched. "He was here. Gabriel took him this way."

Frosty placed a heavy hand on his shoulder, voice deep and solemn. "Then the storm has passed. The true trail begins."

Chapter 17

The Stronghold of Shadows

The trail ended at a chasm that looked like it had been carved into the earth by claws. A bridge of jagged ice stretched across, faintly glowing with veins of red, like an open wound. Beyond it, Gabriel's stronghold rose.

It wasn't a fortress of stone but of corrupted wonder. Once-white towers twisted black, sleigh bells strung like chains, candy-cane arches melted and warped into hooks. And above it all, a crown of dark storm clouds swirled, lightning flashing crimson, as if the very sky bowed to Gabriel's will.

Duke clenched his glowing sword tighter. Frosty's heavy footsteps thumped behind him, and Nico's small voice said, "This must be it."

But before Duke could answer, a wind howled across the bridge. Icy and sharp, like knives of frozen glass. He shielded his eyes, calling out, "Frosty? Nico?"

No answer.

When he lowered his hand, the bridge stretched out empty in front of him. The path behind was gone, swallowed by mist.

"Frosty!" he shouted, panic cracking his voice. "Nico!"

Only silence.

His breath quickened, heart pounding. Alone again. Always alone.

And then Gabriel's voice slithered through the storm. "Did you think they would follow you here, boy? This is between us."

Duke looked across the bridge at the fortress, his jaw tightening. For a moment, fear almost rooted him where he stood. But then he looked down at his hand, the faint hum of his blade pulsing steady, and remembered Santa's words: *"Being Santa is a gift greater than any other."*

He stepped onto the bridge.

Each step echoed like a drumbeat, the wind howling, shadows reaching at his heels. But he didn't stop until the gates of the stronghold stood before him.

They opened on their own, creaking like old bones.

Inside, the air reeked of smoke and melted sugar, the remains of broken toys scattered across the floor like corpses on a battlefield. The halls glowed with a red light that pulsed in rhythm with Duke's own heartbeat.

And at the center, atop a throne of shattered sleigh-wood and twisted wreaths, sat Gabriel. Cloaked in black, his features sharpened like a mirror-dark reflection of Nicholas. His eyes burned the same blue that was once warm in Santa but was now cold and venomous.

Beside him, shackled in chains of shadow, Nicholas knelt. Santa's beard was streaked with ash, his robe torn, but his eyes, gentle and proud, met Duke's across the room.

"Duke…" Santa whispered.

Gabriel rose, his presence filling the chamber like a storm. His voice was silk and thunder all at once.

"You came. Foolish, but expected. Tell me, boy, did Frosty teach you well? Did the toy cheer you on? And yet, here you stand. Alone. Exactly where I wanted you."

Duke's blade sprang to life, glowing brightly, its light casting Gabriel's shadow long across the walls. His fear fluttered in his chest, but he lifted his chin.

"I'm not alone," Duke said, his voice firm. "Not while he's still standing."

Gabriel's smile curled. "Then come, little Santa. Let us see if you're ready to inherit your gift. Or your grave."

The throne room darkened, shadows twisting alive, and the first battle between light and dark truly began.

Chapter 18

Clash of Light and Shadow

The throne room thundered as Gabriel raised his hand. Shadows unravelled from his cloak, swirling into whips of black flame. Duke's blade flared to life, humming loudly, its light cutting through the darkness.

"Come then, boy," Gabriel said, his voice smooth and poisonous. "Show me what Nicholas could never master."

Duke lunged. His blade struck a coil of shadow, sending sparks of ice and light flying across the floor. He struck again and again, pushing forward with all his strength. His speed carried him through the chamber, with streaks of crimson and gold trailing behind like comet fire.

But Gabriel didn't flinch. With a lazy gesture, he redirected Duke's blows, each swing crashing against invisible walls of darkness.

"Fast," Gabriel mused. "But fast means nothing without control."

Duke snarled, his chest burning. He remembered Frosty's lessons, *focus, and restraint*, but rage boiled up, drowning them. He spun, slashing wide arcs, forcing Gabriel back a step.

For a moment, Duke's heart soared. He was holding his own.

Then Gabriel's cloak expanded like wings. Shadow slammed Duke in the chest, hurling him across the hall. He hit the ground hard, his blade skidding from his grip, its light flickering.

Gabriel descended slowly, every step echoing like doom. "Is this Nicholas's heir? A child playing with fire?"

Duke huffed upward, his vision hazy, blood on his lip. His weapon ignited again as he forced himself to stand. "I'm not done!"

He charged again, summoning the *speed of Santa*. In a blink, he was behind Gabriel, blade arcing toward his back, but Gabriel was faster. With a sweep of his hand, he caught Duke mid-strike, the blade trembling in his grip. He twisted, and pain flared through Duke's arm as the weapon sputtered.

"Too predictable," Gabriel whispered in his ear.

The shadows closed around him, suffocating. Duke gasped, his blade dimming. His strength is now gone.

And then–

"DUKE!"

A flash of steel. Nico, tiny and defiant, leapt from the shadows, a toy no longer bound by strings. His wooden sword gleamed as he drove it into Gabriel's hand, breaking the grip. Duke collapsed, coughing, air flooding back into his lungs.

Gabriel staggered a step, more stunned by the audacity than the injury. He freed Nico with a quick flick, sending the toy crashing to the floor.

"Little nuisance," Gabriel growled. His shadows surged, wrapping around Nico like serpents.

"No!" Duke shouted, stumbling toward him.

And then, the storm erupted. Frosty barreled through the side hall, his massive snowy form scattering shadows like shattered glass. He grabbed Gabriel's chains, tearing them apart and freeing Duke for a moment.

"Run, boy!" Frosty roared. "Take Nico and go!"

But Gabriel's eyes narrowed. His cloak surged, a tidal wave of black flame. It engulfed Frosty in an instant. The snowman's roar turned into a muffled cry as his form melted, collapsing into a steaming pool of ice and water.

"FROSTY!" Duke screamed, his heart splitting.

Nico, bruised and cracked, dragged himself upright beside him. "We… we have to move, Duke." His voice shook, yet his eyes burned with determination.

Gabriel stood in the center of the destruction, untouched, his gaze like iron. "Run, hide, cry. It makes no difference. You cannot win. You will break, just as Nicholas broke."

Duke's blade lit again, faint but steady. He stood over Nico, his chest heaving as grief and fury roared within him.

But Frosty's last words echoed in his ears. *Restraint. Restraint, or you fall as Gabriel did.*

With trembling hands, Duke lifted Nico and staggered backward, his eyes locked on Gabriel.

"I'll find a way," Duke whispered. "I'll save Santa… and I'll stop you."

Gabriel's smile curved, cold and cruel. "We'll see."

The shadows rose again, but this time Duke darted through them, carrying Nico, and escaping into the stormy halls, leaving behind the melted remains of Frosty.

Chapter 19

Regroup

The halls of Gabriel's stronghold creaked as if alive. Duke stumbled through them, Nico clutched to his chest, shadows licking at their heels but never quite catching. Finally, they burst out into the open night, collapsing into the snow.

The storm had broken. The sky was clear, stars sharp as diamonds against velvet black. It should have been beautiful, but all Duke could see was the smoking ruin in the distance and the memory of Frosty's last stand.

Duke fell to his knees, setting Nico gently on the ground. His hands shook as he pressed them into the snow, his breath ragged. "He's gone…" he whispered. His voice cracked. "Frosty's gone."

Nico sat up, cracks running through his wooden body. His tiny frame trembled as though each movement might split him apart. "I know," he said softly. "I felt it, too."

The boy clenched his fists, rage and sorrow twisting inside him. His blade pulsed faintly at his side, hungry for release. He wanted to turn back, to face Gabriel again, and to burn every ounce of power he had until the world itself shattered.

But Frosty's words rang louder than his anger. *Restraint.*

Duke slammed his fist into the snow, tears stinging his eyes. "If I were stronger, he wouldn't have—"

"Stop." Nico's voice cut sharply, more than it ever had been. "You can't carry his sacrifice like a burden. Frosty didn't give himself for you to wallow in guilt. He gave himself because he believed in you."

Duke froze, blinking at the tiny figure.

Nico pushed himself to his feet, wobbling but steady. "And… because he knew you'd need this." He reached into his chest, literally, right through the cracked wood, and pulled free a shard of glowing ice. It pulsed with a soft blue light, like a heartbeat.

Duke's eyes widened. "What… what is that?"

Nico cradled it in both hands, reverent. "Frosty's Core. His true self. He must've hidden it in me before we entered the stronghold, just in case." He looked up at Duke, the blue glow painting his carved face. "He wanted you to have it."

The shard thrummed in Duke's palm as Nico placed it there. It was cold, but not painfully so, more like the chill of a fresh snowfall. Power hummed faintly within it, calm and steady.

Duke swallowed hard, the grief in his chest twisting into something else, into resolve.

Nico watched him closely. "There's more, Duke. Something Frosty never told you." He hesitated, his wooden features unreadable. "Gabriel isn't just trying to replace Santa. He wants to corrupt the very magic that fuels Christmas. The 'Christmas Spirit' itself. That's why he's so strong. He's been twisting it, feeding on it."

Duke's breath caught. "So if he wins…"

"There will be no Santa. No joy. No hope. Just endless winter." Nico's voice faltered, but his eyes hardened. "Frosty knew only you could stop that. That's why your training had to push you so far. Why restraint matters more than raw power."

Duke clenched his fist around the shard, feeling its gentle pulse sync with his heartbeat. For the first time, the speed in his veins and the fire in his blade felt… balanced. Not just weapons. Tools. Gifts.

He looked toward the stronghold, smoke still rising into the night. His jaw clenched. "Then I'll finish this. For Frosty. For Santa. For everyone."

Nico, battered but unbroken, nodded. "And you won't do it alone."

For the first time since the storm began, Duke allowed himself a small, determined smile.

Chapter 20

The Hidden Thread

The wind cut sharply against Duke's face as he and Nico moved further away from the stronghold, skirting its shadows. They rested in a hollow beneath a cluster of ice-covered pines, their breath steaming in the cold night.

Nico's cracks had deepened; his joints squeaked as he moved. Still, his carved eyes burned with urgency. "Duke, there's something you need to know. Something Gabriel doesn't want you to understand."

Duke leaned in, clutching Frosty's glowing shard close to his chest. "Tell me."

Nico's wooden fingers tapped nervously against the snow. "You know Gabriel is Santa's brother. But what you don't know is *how* he's been spreading his influence. His power doesn't only come from dark magic. It comes from belief, or rather, from destroying it."

Duke frowned, confused. "Destroying… belief?"

"Yes." Nico's voice lowered, as if the very night might be listening. "Gabriel found a way to twist something new, something humans use every day in your world. It's called the Internet."

The word felt foreign on Duke's tongue. "The Internet?"

Nico nodded gravely. "It's a vast network, threads of light and code, that connects people across the world. They share stories, messages, and even lies. Gabriel has been whispering through it, spreading doubt, fueling the idea that Santa is nothing but a myth. The more children stop believing, the weaker Nicholas becomes. And the stronger Gabriel grows."

The realization hit Duke like a blow. His chest tightened, and the shard in his hand dimmed for a moment. "So that's why the village burned. That's why Santa vanished. It's not just about him, it's about *everyone*. Every child in the world."

Nico's carved face darkened. "Exactly. Gabriel doesn't need to set every house on fire. He only needs to plant the seed of doubt. Doubt spreads faster than any flame."

Duke clenched his fists, the snow beneath him melting from the heat radiating off his blade-hand. "And if he convinces the whole world…"

"…then Christmas dies forever," Nico finished.

The boy's pulse thundered in his ears. He thought of the dream he'd had, the voice in the mirror, the dark reflection calling him *my son*. For the first time, he realized it wasn't just a vision. It was a warning. Gabriel wasn't just trying to destroy Nicholas. He was trying to shape Duke. To twist him with the same lies and hunger for power.

Frosty's words echoed again. *Restraint. Joy, not rage.*

Duke looked up at the sky, stars spread out like snowflakes. "Then we have to stop him. Not just in battle, but in the way he spreads his poison. We have to restore the world's belief."

Nico's carved lips curled into the faintest smile. "Frosty would've been proud to hear you say that."

The shard pulsed brighter in Duke's palm, syncing with the beat of his heart. For the first time, he felt not just like a boy training to be Santa's heir but like someone bearing the weight of the world's joy on his shoulders.

And Gabriel, far away, surely felt it too.

Chapter 21

The Shadow Broadcast

Far beneath the jagged cliffs of the North Pole, in a fortress carved from obsidian ice, Gabriel sat upon a throne of frozen stone. The walls pulsed with a strange bluish light, not from torches but from mirrors. Dozens of them, and all shimmering with moving images.

Children's bedrooms. Classrooms. Television sets. Movie screens. Laptops glowing in the night. Phones held close to tired faces.

Gabriel's dark eyes glowed as he whispered into the void, his voice spilling through the mirrors like poisoned honey.

They want to believe. But what if the truth is simpler? What if the truth is… There is no Santa Claus?

Each whisper rippled outward, not into the wind, but through wires and signals, traveling via satellites orbiting the globe. His magic had merged with the Internet, turning human technology into a vessel for his lies.

On one mirror, a group of men in sharp suits sat around a table in a tall city tower. Their voices buzzed through the glass.

"Kids are growing out of Santa earlier than ever," one said. "It's time we push reality, movies about how Santa's fake, how it's all parents. That'll sell."

Another leaned back, smirking. "We control the stories. We control the belief."

Gabriel's smile was razor-thin. He raised his hand, and shadows poured from his fingers, seeping into the screen. The executives blinked, their eyes flashing with faint black rings. They were no longer men, but puppets.

"Make your films," Gabriel murmured. "Make them laugh at him. Make them doubt him. Every ticket sold, every child who nods and says *Of course he's not real…* that is my victory."

The mirrors shifted again. Now, classrooms flickered across the walls. A teacher stood at a chalkboard, shaking her head at the wide-eyed faces of her students.

"No, children, Santa Claus isn't real. It's just a story parents tell you."

Gabriel's chuckle resonated through the ice chamber, deep and victorious. "One voice becomes many. Many voices become a chorus. Soon belief will wither like frost beneath flame."

At the center of the room stood an object, cloaked in cloth and chained with iron. Gabriel's hand caressed the chains, and beneath the cover a faint, steady glow pulsed like a heartbeat. Nicholas was alive but weakening.

Gabriel whispered to the imprisoned light. "Do you feel it, brother? Every child who doubts you is another shackle on your soul. They will forget you. And then, when they look for joy, they will only find me."

For a moment, his eyes flicked toward one mirror, where a boy's face appeared, sweating in the cold but standing firm. Duke. His blade-hand glowed, his small frame burning with the energy of belief.

Gabriel's smirk faltered. "Still holding on, but not for long."

The mirrors flickered, and hundreds of voices overlapped: laughter at jokes mocking Santa, skeptical parents confessing the "truth," screenplays being written in which Santa was nothing more than a clumsy old man in costume.

And Gabriel drank it all in like wine.

Chapter 22

The Cracks in Belief

Duke sat cross-legged in the snow outside Frosty's cave, his breath steaming in the cold air. The storm was over, but the silence pressed down on him, heavier than any blizzard. His weapon—light flickering from his palm—hummed softly, both comforting and burdensome.

But then… it faltered.

The glow stuttered like a candle in the wind, and his heart dropped. His power was tied to something deeper—something he could feel unraveling far beyond the North Pole.

He clenched his fists. *What's happening to me?*

Nico rested nearby, his little frame battered from their last trial, stitching himself back together with twine and bits of magic Frosty had given him before their separation. His wooden eyes lifted to Duke, worry flickering in their painted shine.

"You feel it too, don't you?" Nico's voice was low.

Duke nodded. "It's like… the joy is slipping away. Not just here. Everywhere."

The toy soldier shuffled closer. "Gabriel is feeding on disbelief. Every child who stops believing in Nicholas and Santa weakens you. Weakens all of us. It's his greatest weapon."

Duke's chest tightened. He thought of the dream—the burning houses, Santa fallen, the mocking voice calling him *son*. Was this it? Was Gabriel winning already?

He slammed his hands into the snow, frustration boiling over. "I can fight monsters. I can face trials. But how do you fight disbelief? How do you fight something you can't even see?"

The snow glittered with the fading hum of his blade-hand. The truth pressed against him like frost seeping into his bones. He was powerful—Frosty had said so. But what good was power when Gabriel was poisoning the entire world with lies?

Nico placed a small hand on Duke's knee. "You don't fight disbelief with force. You fight it by being proof. By being the spark that can't be put out."

Duke closed his eyes, steadying his breathing. He remembered the laughter of the children during the snowball fight, the warmth of Mrs. Claus's table, and the way Santa's voice had carried love even as secrets shadowed it.

Joy. That was the real weapon.

The hum returned, faint at first, then brighter, flowing into his veins. His hand lit with renewed fire, no longer trembling.

But he still couldn't shake the weight pressing down on him — the sensation that Gabriel's influence was extending into every part of the world.

If I fail, Duke thought, staring into the distance, *then Santa isn't the only one who disappears. Joy itself dies with him.*

Chapter 23

Secrets in the Snow

The North Pole was never truly quiet, not even in stillness. The ice cracked somewhere in the distance. A wind whispered along the edges of the cave mouth. And yet, to Duke, it felt like the entire world had gone silent, waiting for him to make the next move.

He leaned back against the cold cave wall, still shaken from his fading power. The blue-white glow that once pulsed from his palm had dimmed, leaving only faint flickers. Nico sat across from him, his small wooden frame propped on a rock, legs dangling. His painted face was steady, but something in his wooden eyes looked older than Duke had ever noticed before.

"Tell me the truth, Nico," Duke said finally, breaking the silence. "You knew things before I did. About Gabriel. About the disbelief spreading. About what's happening to me. How?"

Nico tilted his head, gears inside his chest clicking softly. "Because I wasn't just made to be a toy."

The words hung heavy. Duke leaned forward.

"Then what are you?"

"I was made to watch over you," Nico said quietly. His voice was a careful balance of pride and sorrow. "Not just you, Duke… but whoever would be chosen next. Nicholas always knew his brother might one day rise again. So, he built me—not from wood alone, but from pieces of his own magic."

Duke blinked. "Santa… built you?"

Nico's wooden smile faltered. "Nicholas, yes. He gave me life, memory, and purpose. That's why I know things you don't. That's why I can feel the threads of joy unraveling, just like he can. I was meant to guide, not lead; to protect, not fight. That's why I almost didn't survive the monster. I was never meant to."

Duke's stomach twisted. He had thought of Nico as a friend, a companion in the journey. To realize he was more like a guardian left behind by Santa himself made the air feel colder.

"So, you were never just a toy soldier," Duke whispered.

Nico shook his head. His painted smile was chipped, revealing raw wood beneath. "No. I was made to carry his voice when he could not be there. To remind you what you're meant to be, even when the world tells you otherwise. Nicholas… he feared what Gabriel would do. He feared what Gabriel had already become. So, he poured hope into me. A piece of himself, locked in my chest."

Duke's heart pounded. "And what happens when that piece runs out?"

Nico hesitated. His wooden eyes darkened. "Then I break. And there will be nothing left of me but splinters."

The silence returned, heavier than before. Duke swallowed hard, staring into the dim glow of his hand. "Then I can't let that happen."

Nico chuckled softly, though the sound was brittle. "It's not your choice, Duke. My path is tied to his. To Santa's. And maybe… to yours."

Duke clenched his fist, sparks of blue fire briefly returning. "Then I'll make sure none of us breaks. Not Santa. Not you. Not joy itself."

The toy soldier tilted his head, regarding Duke with something almost like pride. "You're speaking like Nicholas now."

Chapter 24

The Prophecy of Belief

The fire Duke had sparked in his palm faded again, but the warmth lingered between him and Nico. The boy waited, eyes fixed on the small wooden soldier, sensing that something heavier still pressed behind his words.

Nico's painted jaw tightened. The gears inside his chest gave a low, sorrowful hum.

"Duke… Nicholas feared something long before Gabriel broke away. He told me once, in a voice quieter than falling snow: *'The greatest enemy of Christmas is not hatred, nor greed—it is disbelief.'"*

Duke frowned. "Disbelief?"

"Yes," Nico said, his voice grave. "Joy, magic, and even the strength of Santa himself all draw power from belief. From the wonder of children, the hope of families, and the spark that tells the world there is still good worth waiting for. Nicholas feared that if Gabriel turned away, he would strike not at the North Pole, not at Santa directly… but at belief itself."

Duke's breath caught. "And he was right."

Nico nodded slowly. "Gabriel found ways to poison the well. To plant doubt, to whisper lies, to make the world laugh at what it once cherished. The Internet is only the newest weapon he wields. But Nicholas foresaw even this. He feared that one day the North Pole would not fall because it was destroyed, but because no one cared, it was gone."

The boy's stomach sank. He remembered the dream—the burning houses, the voice whispering, "My son"—and a shiver crawled down his spine.

Nico leaned forward, his small frame creaking with each movement. "That's why you matter, Duke. Nicholas knew someone new would rise when belief began to wane. Someone untested, young, still filled with the spark Gabriel lost. That someone is you."

"But…" Duke's voice cracked. "I'm not ready. You saw what happened out there. I almost lost you. I almost failed."

"You *will* fail," Nico said bluntly. "Many times. That is the nature of becoming Santa. Nicholas failed too. Gabriel failed the worst of all. But it is what you do after failure that matters."

Duke clenched his fists. The air around him hummed faintly, threads of blue light flickering like auroras across his arms. For a moment, he felt both hope and terror coil in his chest.

"Tell me, Nico," he whispered. "What exactly did Nicholas fear would happen… if belief fell completely?"

The toy soldier hesitated. Then, in a voice barely above a whisper, he said:

He feared that Gabriel would not only rule the world but also make his version of truth the only reality. A place where joy is ridiculed, wonder is wiped out, and hope is banned—a world where no child dares to dream again.

Duke's breath trembled. He thought of the laughter of his snowball fights, of Mrs. Claus's cookies, of Santa's warm hand on his shoulder—and of how easily it could all vanish.

"I won't let that happen," Duke said, his voice steady now. "Not while I'm here. Not while Nicholas still breathes."

Nico tilted his head, eyes glinting faintly in the cave's light. "Then you must prepare, Duke. Because Gabriel will not stop until belief itself bows to him. And the closer you draw to Nicholas, the darker the trials will become."

Chapter 25

The Trial of Shadows

The snow had eased, leaving the world hushed, silver under the moonlight. Duke and Nico trudged through the drifts; the toy soldier perched on the boy's shoulder like a sentinel. Their breaths mingled with the frost, yet an unease hung in the air, thicker than the cold.

"Something's wrong," Nico murmured. His gears clicked softly, as if straining to hear.

Duke slowed down. The snow under his boots stopped crunching — it now whispered, muttered, and seemed to carry voices that weren't there. Then, in the whiteness ahead, shapes started to form. Children. Dozens of them.

They stood in rows, pale, hollow-eyed. Boys and girls with blank faces, their mouths forming words Duke could not hear. Yet as the wind shifted, he caught it.

There is no Santa.

The words echoed like a chant.

Duke's chest tightened. "This is another one of Gabriel's tricks."

"Not just a trick," Nico said grimly. "A test. Gabriel is attacking the very thing that fuels you—belief."

The children stepped closer, their voices growing louder, overlapping until the chant became a roar.

No Santa. No joy. No hope.

Duke stumbled back, clutching his chest. His powers sputtered, the light fading from his hands. "I can't—when they say it like that, it feels… real."

"That's the trap," Nico urged. His tiny wooden hands gripped Duke's sleeve. "Gabriel doesn't need to kill you. If he makes you doubt yourself, you'll destroy your own strength."

Duke squeezed his eyes shut, but the voices dug in. He saw flashes of himself—ordinary, powerless, just a boy lost in the snow. He heard laughter, cruel and sharp: *Santa isn't real. Neither are you.*

His knees buckled.

"Duke!" Nico barked. "Look at me!"

The boy forced his eyes open. Nico's painted eyes, chipped and scratched from years of wear, glowed faintly with something more than magic. Belief.

"Do you see me?" Nico asked.

"Yes," Duke gasped.

"Then believe. Not in me. Not in Nicholas. Believe in what you've *already done*. You brought light to the snow. You faced the beast without killing it. You held back when rage tempted you. That is what Santa does."

The children's chant rose to a scream, pressing in on all sides.

Duke's breath steadied. His hands trembled—but then the hum of magic returned, flowing through his veins like fire. He pushed back to his feet.

"No," Duke said, his voice shaking but firm. "I *am* real. And so is Santa."

He thrust his hand forward. Light burst from his palm, a flare that cut through the illusions like dawn piercing fog. One by one, the children dissolved into snowflakes, their whispers unraveling into silence.

The world was quiet again.

Duke swayed, exhausted, but standing. "Was... was that real?"

Nico hopped down from his shoulder, boots sinking into the snow. "Real enough. Gabriel wanted to see if you'd break when faced with disbelief. You didn't."

Duke nodded slowly. A grim smile touched his lips. "Then next time, I'll be ready."

But deep inside, a shadow lingered. For even as the illusions faded, he could still hear the faint echo of their chant—*no Santa*—as if Gabriel had planted the seed of doubt not in the snow, but in Duke's own heart.

Chapter 26

The Throne of Shadows

The last echo of the children's whispers died in the wind. The snow stretched silent, unbroken, save for the two figures pressing forward: a boy, and the toy soldier at his side.

Duke's steps felt lighter now, not from exhaustion lifting, but from something new settling in him. The memory of the illusions still burned, but he had beaten them. He had stood tall against doubt.

Nico looked up at him, voice sharp but proud. "That was your first true victory, Duke. Not against claws or fangs, not against fire or storm—but against yourself. Gabriel will try again. He will *always* try. But remember this: you can stand."

Duke nodded. The cold gnawed at his cheeks, but inside, warmth flickered. A steady flame. "I'm not afraid anymore."

"Good," Nico replied, adjusting the strap of his toy musket. "Because we've reached the place where fear is all Gabriel has left."

The snow thinned ahead, giving way to jagged black ice that clawed upward like spears. Beyond it rose a fortress carved into the mountain itself, its spires piercing the storm-heavy sky.

Shadows curled from its walls, twisting like smoke, whispering promises of despair.

The stronghold. Gabriel's throne.

Duke stopped at the edge of the ice field. His breath caught, not in fear this time, but in awe. "So, this is where he's been…"

"Yes," Nico answered grimly. "And where Nicholas is kept."

The boy clenched his fists. Light flickered between his fingers, no longer wild or chaotic, but focused. His weapon—born of pure will—flashed briefly in his hand before vanishing into sparks.

"I'm ready," Duke whispered.

The path forward lit itself with the glow of his resolve. Snow and shadow parted as though bowing to his choice.

Nico looked at him—this boy who only days ago had been playing snowball fights in the yard—and for the first time, the little soldier did not see a child. He saw a Santa in the making.

"Then let us not delay," Nico said, planting his wooden boots firmly in the snow. "Every moment Nicholas remains in chains, Gabriel's lies spread further."

Together, they stepped onto the black ice, toward the fortress.

And deep inside, in the throne room lined with pillars of frozen obsidian, Gabriel stirred. He had sensed the light pierce through his illusions. He had sensed the boy standing.

Gabriel's lips curled into a thin smile. "So, the child chooses to believe."

His voice slithered through the shadows, feeding the darkness that wrapped around him.

"Good. Let him come. Hope tastes sweetest before it dies."

Chapter 27

The Throne Room

The fortress swallowed Duke and Nico the moment they crossed its threshold. Inside, the walls pulsed with a strange black frost, each crystal vein glowing faintly with shadow. Their footsteps echoed in vast corridors where no torches burned, only the eerie glow of despair carved into the stone itself.

Nico kept close to Duke, his musket drawn, though even he admitted it would do little here. "Stay sharp. This place breathes with him."

The air thickened the deeper they went, as though invisible chains were already wrapping around Duke's chest. Each step felt heavier, like the floor was dragging him down into endless night.

Finally, they arrived at a pair of doors—massive slabs of ice-black stone engraved with swirling runes. The carvings glowed faintly, whispering words in a language Duke couldn't understand, yet somehow resonated deep in his bones.

The boy swallowed. "He's in there."

Nico nodded gravely. "Yes. And so is your test."

With a push, the doors opened, groaning like the world itself wept.

The throne room yawned before them—massive pillars of frozen obsidian stretching upward into shadows, no ceiling visible. A carpet of scarlet ice led to a throne carved from a single block of black crystal, jagged and cruel. Upon it sat Gabriel.

He was not hunched like a monster, nor cloaked like some faceless wraith. He was regal, draped in robes of midnight blue trimmed with silver. His beard, dark with streaks of white, framed a face both noble and cold. His eyes gleamed not with malice, but with terrible certainty.

Nicholas was nowhere in sight.

Gabriel's voice rolled through the chamber, calm and resonant, every syllable sinking deep into Duke's chest.

"So, the boy comes. At last."

Duke stepped forward, fists sparking faint light. "Where's Santa? Where's Nicholas?"

Gabriel chuckled, a sound like cracking ice. "Santa…" He spat the name as if it soured his mouth. "Nicholas is weak. He clings to illusions—joy, belief, hope. But you…" His eyes narrowed. "You carry something greater. Something that belongs to me."

Duke felt the shadows pressing closer. His breath grew shallow. "You're wrong. I'm nothing like you."

Gabriel rose from the throne, his height towering, his presence filling every corner of the chamber. He descended the steps slowly, each footfall reverberating like a drumbeat of doom.

"Nothing like me?" he echoed softly. Then, with a sudden sharpness: "Child, *I am you.*"

Duke froze. The light in his hands flickered.

Gabriel's voice deepened, threads of shadow curling around each word. "Why do you think Nicholas took you in? Why do you think he raised you as his own?" His eyes burned with terrible truth. "Because you are mine. My son."

The world tilted. Duke's knees weakened, his weapon sputtering into sparks that scattered uselessly to the ice floor.

"No…" His voice cracked, small, desperate. "That's not true."

But Gabriel pressed closer, towering above him, his words striking like hammer blows.

"Search your heart, boy. Why do you think you dream of me? Why do you think the darkness calls you 'son'? Nicholas feared to tell you—but I, your true father, will not lie."

The boy staggered back. His chest ached, his breath sharp and uneven. The warmth he carried—the flame of belief— flickered low, smothered beneath the weight of Gabriel's truth.

Behind him, Nico shouted, "Duke! Don't listen to him!" but the words sounded far away, drowned in the thunder of Gabriel's revelation.

The shadows rose around the throne, curling into forms— faces of people Duke loved, Mrs. Claus, the villagers, even Nicholas himself—all of them whispering, accusing, vanishing again into the dark.

Gabriel knelt before Duke, lowering his face until their eyes met. His smile was thin, triumphant.

"You are my blood. My heir. You were never meant to save the North Pole, Duke. You were meant to finish my work."

The boy's fists trembled. His light had faded. His heart was shattering.

Chapter 28

The Blood of Winter

Duke stood frozen, the echo of Gabriel's words ringing louder than any storm.

My son.

The chamber seemed to breathe with it. His chest tightened as if invisible chains coiled around his ribs. Every memory of Nicholas, every moment of laughter with Mrs. Claus, every snowball fight under the northern lights — all of it twisted now, distorted, poisoned by Gabriel's revelation.

Duke's voice cracked. "No… Nicholas is my father. He raised me. He—"

"Raised you," Gabriel interjected, his tone sharp but almost pitying. "Yes. But why? Because he couldn't face the truth. He took you from me and hid you behind his false cheer. He tried to shape you into his own image, a sort of mimic of 'Santa.' But you are mine, Duke. My flesh. My shadow. You dream of me because our blood calls across the veil."

The boy's knees buckled, his palms pressed to the icy floor. The cold bit into his skin, yet he could barely feel it — numbness spread through him faster than frost.

"Stop…" he whispered.

Gabriel crouched, his looming figure both regal and monstrous, his hand hovering just above Duke's shoulder. "Why fight what you already know in your heart? The power you wield, the fury that burns when you strike — that is not Nicholas. That is me."

The room darkened, the very walls pulsing with his voice. "Join me, son. Together, we will end this charade of hope. You will surpass Nicholas, surpass even me. We will carve truth into the world — a truth free of illusions. A truth of strength."

Duke's vision blurred. His weapon flickered in his trembling hand, then dimmed to nothing. The fire of Christmas magic sputtered out, smothered under the crushing weight of despair.

He thought of Nicholas — of the warmth in his voice when he tucked him in, the laughter they shared at the supper table. He thought of Mrs. Claus' gentle scolding, the way she called him "our boy." Could all of that be a lie?

A tear slid down his cheek.

Gabriel leaned close, his eyes burning like twin furnaces. "Let go, Duke. Embrace who you truly are. My son."

For a heartbeat, Duke almost surrendered. His fists loosened. His head lowered. His breath trembled on the edge of breaking.

Then — a memory sparked. Nicholas' voice in the quiet of his room, the night he asked if he would be Santa one day:

"Being Santa is a gift, greater than any other… I hope you'll follow in my steps and be greater than I could ever be."

The words flared inside him like an ember refusing to die.

Duke gritted his teeth. His chest still ached, his heart still cracked — but something inside fought back.

"I…" He lifted his head, his eyes burning through tears. "…am not your son."

Gabriel's smile faltered.

Duke stood, legs unsteady but refusing to collapse, sparks of light crackling faintly at his fingertips. "Nicholas is my father. He gave me joy, not despair. He gave me love, not chains. He taught me to give — not to take." His voice steadied, stronger now, cutting through the shadows. "I don't care what blood you think runs in me. I choose *who I am*."

The throne room trembled. A wave of warmth emitted from Duke, subtle but genuine—a glow fighting against the overwhelming darkness.

Gabriel's eyes narrowed. His calm shattered into something harsher, sharper. "So, Nicholas' poison runs deep. Very well."

He rose to his full height, shadows writhing like serpents around him. His voice thundered with fury.

"Then I will break you — and rebuild you in my image."

Chapter 29

Clash of Blood and Light

The throne room trembled as Gabriel unleashed a wave of shadow. Darkness surged forward like a storm, flinging Duke across the icy floor. He hit hard, gasping for breath, but his hand ignited with light before the shadows could consume him.

The blade appeared again — a radiant sword of pure energy, glowing like a star. It pulsed with warmth, steadying his trembling arms.

Gabriel stepped down from his throne, his own weapon forming from the storm — jagged, black, alive with fury. "Do you really think you can stop me, boy? My own blood cannot defeat me."

"I don't want to defeat you," Duke said, his voice shaking but firm. "I want to save you."

Their weapons clashed, light against shadow. Each strike boomed like thunder, sending ripples across the frozen walls. Duke's arms ached, every blow driving him backward, but he pressed on, refusing to fall.

"You don't have to live in this darkness!" he shouted, pushing back with all his strength. "You're not just power. You're not just rage. You're my father."

Gabriel's face tightened, his strikes faltering for a heartbeat. "Do not call me that."

"But it's true," Duke said, his weapon flaring brighter. "And that means I can still believe in you. Even now."

Gabriel's storm roared with anger, yet also hesitation. Shadows whipped fiercely around him, wavering as if even the darkness doubted itself.

"I forgive you," Duke whispered, his voice carrying through the chamber. "For everything."

For a moment, Gabriel froze. The storm cracked. Duke glimpsed something beneath the fury — a man torn apart, not just a villain. His heart clenched with hope.

But then Gabriel's fury returned tenfold. His blade struck with crushing force, shattering Duke's weapon into sparks. The boy collapsed to his knees, the warmth gone, leaving only cold stone beneath his hands.

Gabriel loomed over him, the shadow blade raised high.

"Love will not save you," he hissed. "It will destroy you. And I will show you how."

Chapter 30

The Light Above

Gabriel's shadow blade hovered in the air, its jagged edge trembling inches from Duke's throat. The storm roared behind him, but his hand shook as though the weight of it all pressed against his chest.

"Why… why do you speak of forgiveness?" Gabriel's voice cracked, just barely. His eyes—sharp, burning—wavered. "Do you not see what I've built? What have I become?"

Duke lifted his gaze, bruised and bleeding, but steady. "I see you. Not the monster… the man. My father."

The words echoed through the throne room. Gabriel's blade lowered an inch, shadows pulsing uncertainly. For the first time, Duke saw fear in him—not of power, but of hope.

And in that breath of hesitation, something within Duke broke open. A warmth—no, a current— surged through him, deeper than the magic Frosty had spoken of. Not just speed. Not just light. Something older, boundless.

It lifted him to his feet. His hands glowed not with a blade this time, but with the *Force* itself—pure will, pure love, bending the air around him.

The storm above them split. Through the torn roof of ice, the night sky shimmered. Stars blinked awake. And then, flowing out of Duke's heart, colors painted the heavens: ribbons of emerald, crimson, and gold.

The aurora stretched across the world.

At the North Pole, the villagers, hiding in fear, looked up and gasped.

In warm cities far to the south, children at windows rubbed their eyes, watching the sky dance with shapes—Christmas trees, sleighs, stockings, and the faces of joy they thought were only stories.

Families smiled. Belief stirred. For the first time in years, a spark returned.

Gabriel staggered backward as if struck. "No… what have you done?"

Duke's voice rang, not loud, but confident, carried on the Force itself:

"I won't fight you with anger. I won't fight you with hate. I'll fight you with joy. With love. With everything you tried to erase."

The aurora swirled faster, brighter, filling the sky until even Gabriel's shadows recoiled.

The villain's face twisted, torn between rage and a flicker of something else—pain. His hand shook on his weapon, shadows flickering weakly around him.

But he did not fall.

Not yet.

Chapter 31

The Last Fall

The aurora burned above them, casting colors across Gabriel's ice-forged throne. His shadows sputtered, shrinking against the flood of light. For a heartbeat, Duke thought—*hoped*—he had reached him.

But Gabriel's eyes hardened. The trembling in his hand steadied into rage.

"You think this spectacle can undo me?" His voice thundered, dark power surging in waves. "I am not a tale to be redeemed. I am the storm itself!"

He roared, driving his shadow blade into the frozen floor. A shattering crack split through the throne room. Ice walls groaned, collapsing as fissures spidered outward. The ground buckled beneath their feet, the whole stronghold trembling as if the North Pole itself rejected Gabriel's fury.

Duke staggered, trying to hold his balance as pillars of jagged ice crumbled. Gabriel, standing at the center, lifted his arms—his power lashing wild, a storm turned inward.

The floor gave way.

Gabriel's eyes widened as the ice beneath him split open, plunging into a dark abyss below. He teetered at the edge, shadows clawing at the walls for purchase.

"Father!" Duke shouted, diving forward. His hand shot out, glowing with the Force. Their fingers brushed—Duke straining, muscles burning, trying to pull him back.

Gabriel's face twisted between fury and something else—something Duke had only glimpsed once before: sorrow. His lips trembled as if shaping words too heavy to bear.

"I'm… sorry…"

The sound was fragile, almost broken, before the storm swallowed him whole. Darkness dragged him down, his voice fading into silence, leaving only the echo of what might have been.

The ground sealed itself with a violent crash of ice, sending Duke sprawling onto the fractured floor. The aurora still shimmered above, but it felt hollow now, painted against a sky that no longer answered.

For the first time, the boy who would be Santa felt the weight of victory that tasted like loss.

Chapter 32

Pulled from the Ruins

The ice groaned above, sheets of it threatening to bury Duke where he lay. His breath came in ragged bursts, frost clouding around his lips as the weight of failure pressed heavier than the collapsing stronghold.

"DUKE!"

A small but firm grip latched onto his arm. Nico—battered, his frame cracked from the fight—pulled with surprising strength. "Up, Master Skyrider, before this place becomes your tomb!"

Duke blinked through the haze, forcing himself to rise. Together, they stumbled out of the collapsing chamber, shards of ice crashing behind them like falling bells. The aurora outside still painted the sky in ribbons of light, though now it flickered, as if mourning.

Once safe beyond the stronghold's broken gates, Duke collapsed to his knees in the snow. His fists trembled, glowing faintly with the remnants of the Force he had unleashed. "I had him, Nico. I *had him*. He was right there. I could've—" His voice cracked, "I could've saved him."

Nico knelt beside him, his small porcelain face strangely calm despite the fractures across it. "No, Duke. You did more than any of us could. I saw his eyes when he fell."

Duke turned sharply, hope flickering. "What did you see?"

Nico's glassy eyes softened, almost human. Regret. And… words he did not speak aloud. His lips shaped them even as the abyss claimed him: "*I'm sorry, my son.*"

The wind howled over the snowfields, but for Duke the world went still. He bowed his head, tears stinging, breath shuddering out of him. A storm of emotions surged—anger, grief, but above all, a fragile thread of hope that Gabriel, even in his fall, had not been wholly consumed.

Nico placed a tiny hand on his arm. "Come, Master Skyrider. Your trial is not over. There are still those who need you."

The words jolted Duke upright. He wiped his sleeve across his face, eyes narrowing with purpose. "Santa. Mrs. Claus. We have to find them."

Nico nodded once, then pointed toward the remnants of the stronghold, where the collapse had revealed hidden passageways beneath the ice. "I believe they're held below. That's why Gabriel fought so hard to keep us away from here."

With renewed strength, Duke descended into the caverns, Nico guiding him by torchlight. The tunnels were dark, carved with runes that pulsed faintly with Gabriel's lingering magic. At the deepest chamber, behind bars of frozen crystal, lay Nicholas and Mrs. Claus.

Their eyes widened as Duke rushed forward.

"DUKE!" Mrs. Claus cried, her voice breaking as tears streamed down her cheeks.

Nicholas, though pale and weakened, still carried that familiar warmth in his gaze. "I knew you'd come, son," he said, voice hoarse but steady. "I knew you'd find us."

Duke pressed his hands to the crystal prison. The Force pulsed through him like a heartbeat, brighter than before. With a single surge of will, the frozen bars cracked, then shattered into snow.

Santa and Mrs. Claus stepped free at last, wrapping Duke in an embrace so fierce it melted the cold from his bones.

And for the first time since Gabriel's fall, the boy believed again.

Chapter 33

The First Christmas

For a long while, none of them spoke. Snow drifted through the broken ceiling above, settling gently on their shoulders as Nicholas and Mrs. Claus clung to Duke. The boy buried his face into Mrs. Claus's coat, breathing in the familiar scent of cinnamon and pine, the comfort of home that he feared he'd never feel again.

Nicholas rested a hand on Duke's back, his grip trembling but steady. "You've grown more in these past few days than most do in a lifetime," he whispered. "Through fire and storm, through trials meant to break you—you stood. You carried more sorrow and more weight than any boy should, yet still you fought for joy."

Duke's throat tightened. His mind reeled with everything— the endless trials, the illusions that clawed at his heart, the aching need to find his parents alive, and the crushing truth that his birth father, Gabriel, was gone. He swallowed, but the words splintered as they left him.

"I—I-I tried so hard. I wanted to save them… I wanted to save him. But Gabriel… he was my father. And now—" His voice cracked, breaking beneath grief he could no longer hold.

Mrs. Claus knelt beside him, her eyes shining with tears, her hand warm on his cheek. "We are so sorry, Duke. Sorry for the pain, sorry for what you've had to face. No child should bear what you've borne." Her voice faltered, but her gaze never left his. "And yet—we are proud beyond words. You have given us hope again. You have given the world its light."

Nicholas drew him into a fierce embrace, his beard rough against Duke's temple. "You are not alone. You are loved. By us, and by every heart you've touched. Remember that, always."

The three of them embraced again, the warmth of it pressing against the bitter cold of the cavern. Nico stood at a respectful distance, his cracked porcelain face glowing faintly in the aurora's reflection. For once, his ever-calm eyes betrayed pride.

Two nights later, the North Pole stirred with life once more. The bells, silent through fire and storm, rang again across the village, their chimes carrying hope through the frosted air. Workers and toys bustled, repairing what had been broken, their laughter timid but growing stronger with each passing hour.

On the snowy runway, the sleigh waited—its runners freshly mended, polished until they gleamed beneath the starlight. The reindeer pawed the ground, their breath steaming in the cold, eager to run again.

Duke stood beside Nicholas, still struggling to believe this moment was real. After everything—the battle, the storm,

Gabriel's fall—he was here, about to ride not just in Santa's sleigh, but *with him*.

Nicholas's eyes twinkled as he handed over the reins. "Easy now," he said with that warm, familiar chuckle. "They'll listen to you. Trust them. Trust yourself."

Duke climbed aboard, his hands trembling as he gripped the leather straps. Fear and excitement churned inside him, threatening to overwhelm. Then his fingers brushed against the smooth, cold weight tucked safely in his pocket—Frosty's ancient, icy core. The chill steadied him, reminding him of the friend who had given everything so he could stand here now. Drawing in a breath, Duke tightened his hold on the reins, courage slowly rising through the ache of loss.

With a sharp crack of the reins, the sleigh leapt forward, lifting into the night. The bells sang, the wind rushed, and the aurora summoned once more by Duke's heart flared brighter than ever. Colors rippled across the heavens, forming shapes of joy: children smiling, stockings hung by firelight, gifts waiting under countless Christmas trees.

Duke's chest swelled as they soared higher, faster, the world stretching beneath their flight. He turned to Nicholas, who gave him a proud nod that needed no words.

"This," Santa said at last, his voice carrying through the night air, "is your first Christmas, Duke."

And together, they laughed as the sleigh cut across the sky, spreading joy like sparks of fire into the darkest corners of the world.

Far below, at the edge of a darkened forest where the snow fell heavier, a lone figure stood in the drifts. The aurora shimmered across the heavens above her. Its shapes of joy reflected in her eyes—eyes that glowed faintly, like embers banked in shadow.

The hood of her cloak swallowed her face, the fabric blacker than the winter night. Only the faint outline of her lips caught the light as she whispered words too soft to carry. The wind tugged at her cloak, revealing only a glimpse of pale skin, almost colorless, before the fabric fell back into place.

Her gaze never left the sleigh as it passed overhead. For a heartbeat, the glow of the aurora caught in her eyes—striking, sharp, unblinking.

As the bells faded into the distance, a smile flickered, thin and dangerous. Her voice, low and almost swallowed by the snow, slipped into the stillness.

"…My son."

The End.